Game of Groans:
The Irony Throne

A Tale of Laughter, Unity, and the Power of Puns

By Tim Krimmel

TIM KRIMMEL

Disclaimer

This book is a work of fiction. Names, characters, places, and incidents are the product of the author's imagination or are used fictitiously. Any resemblance to actual events, locales, or persons, living or dead, is entirely coincidental.

The author acknowledges the trademarked status and trademark owners of various products, brands, and creative works referenced in this book. These references are used for the purpose of parody, and no endorsement, sponsorship, or affiliation should be inferred.

This book is intended to entertain and evoke laughter through the use of puns, humor, and parody. It is not meant to be taken seriously or to offend any individuals, groups, or fandoms. If you are a fan of the original work that inspired this parody, please enjoy this book in the spirit of fun and lightheartedness it was written in.

If you are easily offended or do not appreciate puns and humor, this book might not be for you. However, if you choose to continue reading, please do so with an open mind and a sense of humor.

© Copyright 2023 Tim Krimmel

All rights reserved. No part of this book may be used or reproduced in any manner whatsoever without written permission from the author, except in the case of brief quotations embodied in critical articles and reviews.

Happy reading, and may the laughter be ever in your favor!

GAME OF GROANS: THE IRONY THRONE

TIM KRIMMEL

Table of Contents

PROLOGUE: THE AGE OF LAUGHTER — 8

CHAPTER 1: A CLASH OF PUNS — 10

CHAPTER 2: THE PUNDERING BEGINS — 18

CHAPTER 3: A CLASH OF PUNS — 25

CHAPTER 4: THE BATTLE OF WITS — 32

CHAPTER 5: A FEAST FOR LAUGHS — 34

CHAPTER 6: THE LAUGHTER THAT NEVER ENDS — 37

CHAPTER 7: THE FESTIVAL OF FOLLY — 43

CHAPTER 8: SERSILLY LANNIST-HAIR — 47

CHAPTER 9: SQUIRE PYCELLE — 50

CHAPTER 10: SIR JORAH MEMEONT — 52

CHAPTER 11: JON SNOWMAN — 54

EPILOGUE: A REALM UNITED IN LAUGHTER — 56

BONUS CONTENT — 58

GAME OF GROANS: THE IRONY THRONE

TIM KRIMMEL

Prologue: The Age of Laughter

Long before the Irony Throne was forged and the Great Houses of Jesteroos began their comical struggle for power, the realm was united under the banner of laughter, its people bound together by the shared love of humor and wit. In those days, the power of a well-crafted pun could win wars, forge alliances, and bring the most bitter of enemies together in a moment of shared mirth.

It was during this golden age of laughter that the seeds of the Game of Groans were first sown, as the great jesters and pun-masters of the realm began to vie for influence and recognition, their quips and jibes growing ever more elaborate in pursuit of the ultimate punchline. The people of Jesteroos reveled in this age of merriment, their spirits buoyed by the never-ending parade of jests and jokes that filled the air.

Yet, as the laughter grew louder, so too did the whispers of discontent, as the once-simple pleasure of sharing a laugh began to give way to the darker forces of ambition and rivalry. It was then that the first cracks appeared in the realm's once-united facade, as the people of Jesteroos began to divide themselves along the lines of wit and humor, their loyalties tested by the growing demands of the Game of Groans.

And so, the Age of Laughter began its slow descent into the world of petty squabbles and bitter rivalries that would come to define the realm of Jesteroos for generations to come. As the great houses of the realm turned against one another, their laughter curdling into the bitter taste of betrayal, the once-united people of Jesteroos found themselves caught in the crossfire, their joy and mirth sacrificed on the altar of ambition.

Yet, even in the darkest of times, the light of laughter could never be truly extinguished, its flickering embers a constant reminder of the power of humor to heal the wounds of the past and forge a brighter future. As the Irony Throne cast its long shadow over the realm, a new generation of heroes would rise to challenge the forces of darkness and despair, their hearts filled with laughter and their voices raised in defiance.

This is the story of the Game of Groans, a tale of humor and heartache, puns and peril, laughter and loss. It is a story that will span the breadth and depth of Jesteroos, touching the lives of all who call the realm home, and forever altering the course of history. And at its heart lies the eternal truth that laughter, in all its forms, has the power to change the world.

Chapter 1: A Clash of Puns

Neddard Snark

Long before the realm of Jesteroos was united under the banner of laughter and wit, the Snark family ruled over the peaceful and verdant lands of Wintergrin. In those days, the family was known for their solemnity and stoicism, their faces as unyielding as the frozen tundra of the North.

Neddard Snark, the head of the family, was a man of great honor and integrity, admired by his people for his unwavering sense of duty and loyalty. However, Neddard was not known for his sense of humor – in fact, he was often described as being as dour as the winter winds that swept across the lands of Wintergrin.

One fateful day, a wandering minstrel by the name of Petyr "Littlejester" Baelish arrived in Wintergrin, bringing with him tales of laughter and merriment from far-off lands. Intrigued by the strange and unfamiliar sounds of laughter that echoed through the halls of Wintergrin Castle, Neddard invited Littlejester to perform before him and his family.

As the minstrel regaled the Snarks with his tales and jokes, the cold, stern faces of the family began to crack, as laughter – a sound rarely heard in the lands of Wintergrin – filled the air. Neddard found himself bewitched by the power of humor, as it broke down the barriers between him and his people, fostering a newfound sense of camaraderie and warmth.

In the days that followed, Neddard Snark became a changed man. He sought to learn the secrets of humor and wit from Littlejester, who was only too happy to share his knowledge with the Lord of Wintergrin. As the two men spent countless hours honing their craft, a strong bond of friendship was forged between them, one that would change the course of history.

With each passing day, Neddard Snark grew more adept at the art of jesting and wordplay, and soon the halls of Wintergrin Castle were alive with the sounds of laughter and mirth. The people of Wintergrin, once known for their stoicism and solemnity, embraced the joy and warmth that laughter brought to their lives, as the spirit of humor and wit spread throughout the land.

It was during this time that Neddard Snark learned of the looming threat to the realm – the Punder Walkers, who sought to extinguish the light of laughter and plunge the world into an endless winter of silence and despair. Determined to protect his people and the newfound spirit of mirth that had taken root in Wintergrin, Neddard vowed to stand against the Punder Walkers and defend the realm of Jesteroos.

As Neddard Snark's reputation as a master of wit and humor grew, so too did the legacy of the Snark family. No longer known for their stoicism and solemnity, the Snarks became champions of laughter and unity, leading the fight against the Punder Walkers and forging alliances with the other great houses of Jesteroos.

And so, the legend of Neddard Snark was born – a tale of transformation, friendship, and the power of laughter to change the world. The people of Wintergrin would never forget the man who had brought light and warmth to their lives, and his legacy would live on through the generations, as the Snark family continued to uphold the values of humor, unity, and triumph in the face of darkness.

Winterjests

Neddard Snark, Lord of Winterjests and Warden of the Jorth, stared out of his castle's window, watching the arrival of the royal entourage. King Baratheomnomnom and his court were visiting Winterjests, and Neddard couldn't help but feel a sense of foreboding as the procession snaked its way through the snowy landscape. He couldn't quite put his finger on it, but something in the back of his mind told him this visit was the start of a great upheaval in Jesteroos.

"Father, do you think King Baratheomnomnom will bring a jester with him?" asked Robsnark, Neddard's eldest son and heir, unable to contain his excitement.

Neddard chuckled at his son's enthusiasm. "I'm sure he will, Robsnark. His jesters are said to be the most amusing in all of Jesteroos."

Neddard's wife, Caitalyn, entered the room, her expression a mix of worry and amusement. "I just hope he doesn't bring that abominable Queen Sersilly Lannist-hair. The woman is a walking disaster."

Neddard sighed, knowing full well that his wife was right. Queen Sersilly had a reputation for stirring up trouble wherever she went. However, he didn't have the luxury of choosing who accompanied the King.

"Unfortunately, my love, we have no choice but to welcome them all. It's our duty as loyal subjects of the Irony Throne," he said, wrapping his arm around his wife's shoulders.

As the royal procession approached the gates of Winterjests, Neddard and his family stood waiting in the courtyard, surrounded by bannermen, servants, and well-wishers. The gates creaked open, and the royal entourage finally entered the castle.

King Baratheomnomnom dismounted his horse with a great effort, a wide grin on his face. "Neddard! My old friend!" he boomed, his voice echoing through the courtyard. He embraced Neddard in a bear hug that nearly knocked the wind out of him. "It's been far too long!"

"Your Grace, welcome to Winterjests," Neddard replied, his voice slightly strained from the tight embrace. "It's an honor to have you here."

As the King released him, Neddard couldn't help but notice the mischievous gleam in Baratheomnomnom's eyes. He knew that look all too well; it usually meant trouble.

Just then, Queen Sersilly Lannist-hair entered the courtyard, a self-satisfied smirk on her face. Her golden hair was styled in an elaborate mess, and she wore a gown adorned with what appeared to be small bells. As she walked, the bells jingled loudly, drawing the attention of everyone present.

"Ah, Lord Snark," she said, a sly grin on her face. "Your castle is... quaint."

Neddard's jaw clenched at her obvious insult, but he forced himself to remain polite. "Thank you, Your Grace. We do our best to maintain its rustic charm."

The King clapped Neddard on the back, his laughter booming through the courtyard. "Now, now, no need for pleasantries! We're all friends here, aren't we? Come, let us feast and be merry!"

Neddard forced a smile as he led the King and his entourage to the Great Hall, the weight of his worries growing heavier with each step.

The feast was a loud and boisterous affair, with jesters and minstrels performing for the entertainment of the gathered nobles. The Great Hall of Winterjests was filled with laughter and merriment, but Neddard couldn't shake the nagging feeling that the frivolity wouldn't last.

As the evening wore on, King Baratheomnomnom consumed more and more flagons of mead, his laughter growing louder and more raucous with each passing moment. Neddard watched him with concern, unsure of how much more the King could imbibe before making a spectacle of himself.

Meanwhile, Queen Sersilly Lannist-hair held court with a group of nobles, her voice dripping with sarcasm as she shared stories of her time at the capital, Pun's Landing. Each tale seemed more outrageous than the last, and Neddard couldn't help but roll his eyes at her wild exaggerations.

Suddenly, the doors to the Great Hall burst open, and a motley crew of jesters tumbled into the room, their colorful costumes and painted faces drawing the attention of the gathered guests. At the head of the group was a tall, lanky figure with a shock of red hair and an impish grin.

"Lords and ladies of Winterjests," he announced with a flourish, "I present to you the Royal Jester of Pun's Landing, Sir Giggles the Witty!"

The hall erupted in applause as Sir Giggles took the stage, his quick wit and clever wordplay captivating the audience. Even Neddard couldn't help but laugh at the jester's hilarious antics, momentarily forgetting his concerns about the King's visit.

As the evening drew to a close, Neddard found himself cornered by Squire Pycelle, the bumbling Hand of the King. The man's incessant rambling was enough to drive anyone mad, and Neddard couldn't help but wonder how he had managed to secure such a high position in the King's court.

"Lord Snark, I must say, this has been a delightful evening!" Pycelle exclaimed, his words slurred by the copious amounts of mead he had consumed. "And I must confess, I was most impressed by Sir Giggles! He truly is a master of the pun!"

Neddard nodded politely, praying for a swift end to the conversation. "Yes, he is quite the talent."

Just then, King Baratheomnomnom approached, a serious expression on his face. "Neddard, I have a matter of great importance to discuss with you. It concerns the future of Jesteroos and the Irony Throne."

Neddard felt a chill run down his spine, his earlier worries returning in full force. "Of course, Your Grace. We can speak privately in my study."

The two men left the Great Hall, leaving the sounds of laughter and merriment behind them. As they entered Neddard's study, the King closed the door and turned to face him, his expression grave.

"Neddard, my old friend," he began, his voice heavy with the weight of his words. "Jesteroos is in peril. There are those who seek to undermine my rule and usurp the Irony Throne. I need your help to put an end to their schemes and restore order to the realm."

Neddard felt his heart sink at the King's words, but he knew he had no choice but to offer his assistance. "Your Grace, you have my unwavering loyalty. Whatever you need, I am at your service."

King Baratheomnomnom nodded, his eyes filled with gratitude. "Thank you, Neddard. Together, we will ensure that Jesteroos remains a land of laughter and joy."

As Neddard pledged his allegiance to the King, he couldn't help but feel a sense of unease. He knew that the path ahead would be fraught with danger and intrigue, but he was determined to do whatever it took to protect Jesteroos and its people from the looming threat.

Meanwhile, at the far end of the world, in the sun-scorched land of Es-Slack, a young woman with silver hair and eyes like amethysts gazed out at the horizon, her heart filled with determination. Danyslack Targroan, the last remaining heir of the once-great House Targroan, was preparing to embark on a journey that would change the course of history.

With her loyal companion, Sir Jorah Memeont, at her side, Danyslack plotted her return to Jesteroos and the Irony Throne that was rightfully hers. She had heard whispers of a secret weapon that could bring her enemies to their knees—a brood of rubber chickens with powers beyond imagination.

As the sun set over Es-Slack, Danyslack and Sir Jorah Memeont set off on their quest, their hearts filled with hope and their minds focused on the task at hand. The Irony Throne would be theirs, and Jesteroos would once again know the rule of the Targroans.

Back in Winterjests, Neddard's youngest son, Rico Snark, wandered the castle's dimly lit corridors, his curiosity piqued by the strange noises emanating from the King's quarters. He pressed his ear to the door, straining to hear what was happening inside.

Much to his surprise, he heard the unmistakable sounds of laughter and merriment. Unable to contain his curiosity, he cracked open the door, just enough to catch a glimpse of the revelry within.

To his amazement, he saw King Baratheomnomnom and his entourage engaged in a wild pillow fight, feathers flying through the air like a blizzard of white. The sight was so absurd that Rico Snark couldn't help but laugh, drawing the attention of the King and his guests.

"Ah, young Rico Snark!" the King bellowed, a wide grin on his face. "Why don't you join us in our festivities?"

Despite the absurdity of the situation, Rico Snark couldn't resist the King's invitation. He entered the room and joined the fray, his laughter mingling with that of the others as they waged their epic pillow battle.

As the night wore on, the sounds of laughter and merriment echoed through the halls of Winterjests, a snark contrast to the mounting tension and looming danger that threatened the realm. And as the battle for the Irony Throne began to unfold, the people of Jesteroos would soon discover that the line between laughter and tears was thinner than they could have ever imagined.

Thus began the saga of the Game of Groans, a tale of puns and power, laughter and loss, and the eternal struggle for control of the Irony Throne.

Chapter 2: The Pundering Begins

King Baratheomnomnom

In the days before the unification of Jesteroos under the banner of laughter, the lands to the south were ruled by House Baratheomnomnom. Known for their insatiable appetites and love for feasting, the Baratheomnomnoms were a force to be reckoned with, both at the dinner table and on the battlefield.

The most famous member of this proud and gluttonous house was King Baratheomnomnom, a larger-than-life figure who was as renowned for his culinary prowess as he was for his martial skill. Born into a life of privilege and excess, King Baratheomnomnom was raised on a steady diet of lavish feasts and sumptuous banquets, honing his skills as a gourmand and a warrior.

As a young man, King Baratheomnomnom traveled the realm, seeking out the finest ingredients and culinary secrets to add to his already impressive repertoire. Along the way, he crossed paths with a wandering chef by the name of Jamie Lan-nom-ster, who introduced him to the world of cooking puns and food-based wordplay.

Intrigued by the playful and lighthearted nature of culinary humor, King Baratheomnomnom became a student of Jamie Lan-nom-ster, learning the art of cooking puns and food-based wordplay. Together, the two men forged a powerful and lasting friendship, united by their shared love of food and laughter.

As the years went by, King Baratheomnomnom continued to expand his culinary empire, establishing a network of feast halls and banquet venues throughout the realm. He became known as a generous and benevolent ruler, sharing his wealth and culinary expertise with his subjects, who came to love and respect their gluttonous king.

However, King Baratheomnomnom's life was not without its share of tragedy and loss. His beloved wife, Queen Margarine Tyrell, passed away unexpectedly, leaving him heartbroken and bereft. In his grief, King Baratheomnomnom turned to food for solace, his once-healthy appetite spiraling out of control.

It was during this dark period that King Baratheomnomnom heard of the Festival of Folly, a week-long celebration of laughter and mirth in the lands to the north. Desperate to find a way to heal his broken heart, King Baratheomnomnom traveled to Pun's Landing, where he hoped to find solace and joy amidst the laughter and merriment of the festival.

As King Baratheomnomnom immersed himself in the festivities, he found himself drawn to the world of jesting and wordplay, as he recognized the same playful spirit that had captivated him during his culinary adventures with Jamie Lan-nom-ster. Inspired by the power of laughter to heal and unite, King Baratheomnomnom made a vow to bring the spirit of the Festival of Folly back to his own lands.

Returning to his kingdom, King Baratheomnomnom set about transforming his realm into a haven of laughter and mirth. He established jesting academies, where aspiring pun-masters and jesters could hone their craft, and commissioned the construction of grand feast halls, where the people could gather to share food, laughter, and stories.

As the spirit of laughter and mirth spread throughout the lands of House Baratheomnomnom, the people found themselves united by a shared love of food and humor. And as the legacy of King Baratheomnomnom continued to grow, so too did the bonds of friendship and unity between his people, creating a realm where laughter and feasting reigned supreme.

King Baratheomnomnom's transformation of his realm did not go unnoticed by the other great houses of Jesteroos. As word of the Baratheomnomnom's legendary feasts and celebrations spread, emissaries from across the realm traveled to witness the spectacle for themselves. It was during one such feast that King Baratheomnomnom met Neddard Snark, the Lord of Wintergrin, and the two men quickly became friends, bonding over their shared love of humor and their desire to bring laughter to their people.

As the friendship between King Baratheomnomnom and Neddard Snark grew, so too did the ties between their houses, forging an alliance that would prove instrumental in the fight against the Punder Walkers. United by their love of laughter and the power of humor, the houses of Baratheomnomnom and Snark stood side by side, ready to face the darkness that threatened the realm of Jesteroos.

In the years that followed the defeat of the Punder Walkers, King Baratheomnomnom continued to rule over his lands with a generous and open hand, sharing his love of feasting and humor with all who visited his realm. He became a symbol of the power of laughter to heal and unite, his legendary feasts and banquets drawing people from across the realm to partake in the joy and merriment of the Baratheomnomnom table.

As the legacy of King Baratheomnomnom continued to grow, so too did the bonds of friendship and unity between the great houses of Jesteroos. Together, they stood as a testament to the power of laughter and the indomitable spirit of the people, creating a realm where humor and mirth reigned supreme.

And as the people of Jesteroos continued to laugh and share their stories, the memory of King Baratheomnomnom lived on, a reminder of the power of laughter to heal, unite, and transform even the most broken of hearts. His love of food and humor would become an integral part of the Jesteroos culture, ensuring that the legacy of the Baratheomnomnom house would endure for generations to come.

Beyond the Wall of Laughter

In the frozen wastelands beyond the Wall of Laughter, Jon Snowman stood atop the icy barrier, his eyes scanning the horizon for any sign of the dreaded Punder Walkers. As a member of the Night's Chuckle, it was his duty to protect Jesteroos from the terrible puns and wordplay that these creatures wielded like deadly weapons. Little did he know that an even greater threat lurked in the shadows, waiting to strike.

Back in Winterjests, Neddard Snark gathered his family in the Great Hall, preparing to share the grave news that King Baratheomnomnom had entrusted to him. The room was silent as Neddard took a deep breath and began to speak.

"My family, I have been given a heavy burden by our King. There are those who seek to undermine his rule and claim the Irony Throne for themselves. It is our duty to stand by our King and protect the realm from this threat."

His children exchanged worried glances, unsure of what this meant for their family and the future of Jesteroos. Neddard's wife, Caitalyn, placed a hand on his arm, her eyes filled with concern.

"Neddard, what must we do?" she asked, her voice barely more than a whisper.

"We must be vigilant," Neddard replied, his voice steady and strong. "We must stand together, as a family, and do whatever it takes to ensure the safety of Jesteroos."

His family nodded in agreement, their expressions filled with determination. They knew that the path ahead would be difficult, but they were prepared to face whatever challenges lay before them.

In the distant land of Es-Slack, Danyslack Targroan and Sir Jorah Memeont continued their quest for the fabled rubber chickens. Their journey had taken them through treacherous terrain and deadly deserts, but they remained undeterred, their resolve unwavering.

One day, as they traversed the sun-scorched sands of the Giggling Wastes, they stumbled upon a mysterious cave, its entrance hidden beneath a pile of ancient joke books. As they carefully pushed the tomes aside, the cave's entrance was revealed, and a strange, eerie laughter echoed from within.

Danyslack exchanged a nervous glance with Sir Jorah, her heart pounding with anticipation. Could this be the resting place of the legendary rubber chickens?

With cautious steps, they entered the cave, the laughter growing louder and more unsettling with each passing moment. The walls of the cave were lined with shelves, each filled with a bizarre assortment of comical artifacts and trinkets.

And then, as they rounded a corner, they found it — a nest of rubber chickens, their beady eyes staring up at them with a mixture of curiosity and amusement.

Danyslack's eyes widened in awe, her heart swelling with hope. "Sir Jorah, we've found them! With these rubber chickens, the Irony Throne will be ours!"

But as she reached out to take one of the rubber chickens, a voice echoed through the cave, its tone ominous and chilling.

"Who dares disturb the slumber of the Punder Master?" the voice boomed, causing the very walls of the cave to tremble.

Danyslack and Sir Jorah exchanged a fearful glance, realizing that their quest was far from over. To claim the rubber chickens and secure the Irony Throne, they would first have to face the dreaded Punder Master—a being of unimaginable wordplay and wit.

As they steeled themselves for the battle ahead, the Punder Master emerged from the shadows, a tall, cloaked figure with a twisted smile that sent shivers down their spines. The Punder Master raised a bony hand, and with a flick of his wrist, a barrage of terrible puns filled the air, threatening to overwhelm Danyslack and Sir Jorah.

"Enough!" Danyslack shouted, her voice ringing out with authority. "We have come for the rubber chickens, and we will not leave without them!"

The Punder Master's twisted smile widened, and he let out a sinister laugh. "Very well, Targroan. If you seek the power of the rubber chickens, you must first best me in a battle of wits and wordplay. Prepare yourself, for the Pundering is about to begin!"

Danyslack and Sir Jorah braced themselves for the onslaught, their minds racing as they tried to come up with puns of their own. The cave echoed with the sounds of their verbal sparring, each pun more outrageous and groan-inducing than the last.

Back in Winterjests, Neddard's youngest daughter, Arya Snark, was struggling to find her place in the rapidly changing world around her. As her family prepared for the battle against the Irony Throne's usurpers, Arya longed for something more than the life of a noble lady.

One day, as she wandered the castle's training yard, she stumbled upon a mysterious figure practicing with a wooden sword. Intrigued, Arya approached the stranger, her curiosity piqued.

"Who are you?" she asked, her voice filled with wonder.

The stranger turned to face her, revealing a mischievous smile and a twinkle in his eye. "I am Syri-Haha Forel, master of the Comedic Dance. And you, young Snark, have the look of someone who wishes to learn my ways."

Arya's eyes widened in awe, and she nodded eagerly. "Yes! Please, teach me how to fight with laughter and wit!"

And so, under the tutelage of Syri-Haha Forel, Arya began her training in the Comedic Dance, learning the art of combining humor and swordplay in a dazzling display of skill and wit. As she honed her abilities, she dreamed of the day when she could join her family in their fight for the Irony Throne, using her newfound talents to defend Jesteroos from the forces of darkness.

As the battle for the Irony Throne continued to unfold, the people of Jesteroos found themselves caught in a whirlwind of laughter, tears, and terrible puns. But through it all, they held onto the hope that one day, the Irony Throne would be secured, and peace would return to their land.

For in the Game of Groans, you laugh or you cry — there is no middle ground.

Chapter 3: A Clash of Puns

Danyslack Targroan

In the far-off lands of Exile-isle, the once-mighty House Targroan lived in relative obscurity, their once-glorious legacy reduced to a distant memory. Among the surviving members of this fallen house, Danyslack Targroan, a young woman of humble origins, dared to dream of a brighter future for her family.

Born to the Mad King and his wife, Danyslack was the youngest of the Targroan siblings. As a child, she was regaled with stories of her family's glorious past, tales of dragon-riding ancestors who had once ruled the skies and the lands of Jesteroos with an iron grip. But the fall of House Targroan had left them with nothing but memories and a bitter longing for the power they had once wielded.

As Danyslack grew older, she became determined to restore her family's name and reclaim their place among the great houses of Jesteroos. However, she recognized that the ways of her ancestors, built on fear and domination, would never bring lasting peace or happiness to her people.

Inspired by the laughter and mirth that united the realm during the Festival of Folly, Danyslack sought to learn the art of humor and wordplay, believing that the power of laughter could be the key to her family's redemption. She traveled the lands of Exile-isle, seeking out the most skilled jesters and pun-masters, and studied under their tutelage.

In her quest for knowledge, Danyslack encountered a mysterious man named Jorahtoo Mormuch, a wandering bard with a penchant for puns and riddles. Jorahtoo recognized in Danyslack a kindred spirit and a fierce determination to bring joy and laughter to the people of Jesteroos. Together, they embarked on a journey to reclaim the lost legacy of House Targroan, one laugh at a time.

As Danyslack honed her skills in humor and wit, she found herself drawn to the stories of the mythical Punder Dragons, creatures of immense power and wisdom whose very breath could ignite the spark of laughter. Believing that these creatures held the key to her family's future, Danyslack set out to find the fabled Punder Dragon eggs, hidden away in a secret location known only to the most devoted pun-masters.

After years of searching, Danyslack and Jorahtoo finally discovered the hidden cache of Punder Dragon eggs. As she held the eggs in her hands, Danyslack felt a surge of warmth and power, as if the very essence of laughter and joy was coursing through her veins. In that moment, she knew that she was destined to become the Mother of Punder Dragons, a leader who would unite the realm of Jesteroos through the power of humor and the magic of laughter.

Returning to Exile-isle with the precious eggs, Danyslack began the arduous process of hatching the Punder Dragons, using her newfound skills in humor and wit to awaken the dormant creatures. As the first of the Punder Dragons emerged from its shell, Danyslack felt a profound connection to the creature, sensing the potential for a new era of laughter and unity for her people.

With the Punder Dragons at her side, Danyslack Targroan set her sights on Jesteroos, determined to reclaim her family's legacy and bring laughter and joy to a realm beset by darkness and despair. And as the Mother of Punder Dragons prepared to embark on her quest, the people of Exile-isle rallied behind her, their spirits buoyed by the promise of a brighter, more laughter-filled future for all.

As word of Danyslack's Punder Dragons spread throughout the realm of Jesteroos, the other great houses began to take notice. While some viewed her as a threat, others saw in her a potential ally, a unifying force that could bring an end to the centuries-old rivalries and petty squabbles that had long plagued the realm.

Danyslack and Jorahtoo, accompanied by their loyal followers and the powerful Punder Dragons, set sail for Jesteroos, eager to forge new alliances and reclaim the Targroan legacy. In her heart, Danyslack knew that the road ahead would be fraught with challenges and dangers, but she remained steadfast in her belief that laughter and humor could overcome even the darkest of obstacles.

As they approached the shores of Jesteroos, Danyslack and her followers prepared themselves for the trials that lay ahead. With the Punder Dragons at her side and the power of laughter in her heart, Danyslack Targroan stood ready to face whatever challenges the Game of Groans might throw at her, determined to restore her family's name and bring a new era of unity and mirth to the realm of Jesteroos.

The story of Danyslack Targroan serves as a testament to the transformative power of humor and the resilience of the human spirit. In her journey from obscurity to the Mother of Punder Dragons, Danyslack proves that laughter can bridge the gap between the past and the future, uniting the realm in the face of adversity and setting the stage for a brighter, more laughter-filled world.

Pun's Landing

In the heart of Pun's Landing, the capital city of Jesteroos, Tyrione Lannist-haha, the Imp of the Lannist-hair family, sat in his study, pondering the current state of the realm. He had always been known for his quick wit and sharp tongue, but the growing tension between his family and the Snarks of Winterjests weighed heavily on his mind.

As he sipped from his goblet of mead, he couldn't help but wonder if there was a way to bring peace to Jesteroos without resorting to all-out war. With a sigh, he turned his attention to the stack of parchment on his desk, searching for answers within their ink-stained pages.

Meanwhile, in the icy wastelands beyond the Wall of Laughter, Jon Snowman and his fellow members of the Night's Chuckle faced a terrifying new threat. Reports had reached them of Punder Walkers growing in number, their puns more powerful and fearsome than ever before. Jon knew that time was running out, and he needed to find a way to stop the Punder Walkers before they unleashed their terrible wordplay upon the unsuspecting realm of Jesteroos.

As he stood atop the Wall of Laughter, Jon's thoughts turned to his family in Winterjests. He longed to be with them, to stand by their side in the fight for the Irony Throne. But he knew that his duty lay with the Night's Chuckle, and he couldn't abandon his post while the threat of the Punder Walkers loomed large.

In Es-Slack, the battle of wits between Danyslack Targroan and the Punder Master raged on, neither side willing to concede defeat. The air was thick with the tension of their verbal sparring, each pun more audacious than the last.

As the Punder Master unleashed a particularly groan-worthy pun, Danyslack felt her resolve faltering. She turned to Sir Jorah Memeont, her eyes filled with desperation.

"Sir Jorah, I don't know if I can keep this up," she whispered, her voice trembling. "What if I fail?"

Sir Jorah placed a reassuring hand on her shoulder, his expression filled with determination. "Your Grace, you are the last Targroan, the rightful heir to the Irony Throne. I know you have the strength and wit to best this Punder Master. You must believe in yourself."

With renewed resolve, Danyslack turned back to face the Punder Master, her mind racing as she prepared to deliver the final, decisive pun that would secure their victory.

Back in Winterjests, Arya Snark continued her training with Syri-Haha Forel, each day bringing her closer to mastering the Comedic Dance. As she parried and riposted with her wooden sword, her laughter echoed through the training yard, her heart filled with joy and purpose.

As the sun began to set, Arya paused in her training, her gaze drawn to the distant horizon. Somewhere out there, her family was fighting for the Irony Throne, and she longed to join them. But she knew that she had to complete her training, to become the skilled and witty warrior that Jesteroos needed.

As the people of Jesteroos braced themselves for the coming storm, the battle for the Irony Throne continued to escalate. In a realm where laughter and tears were as deadly as steel, the struggle for power would be a test of wit and resilience unlike any they had ever faced before.

For in the Game of Groans, laughter was the only weapon that could cut through the darkness, and only those with the sharpest wit and the most unbreakable spirit would emerge victorious.

In Pun's Landing, Tyrione Lannist-haha poured over books and scrolls, seeking a diplomatic solution to the escalating conflict. He believed that the key to peace lay in uniting the families of Jesteroos through laughter, rather than bloodshed. As he studied late into the night, an idea began to take shape in his mind—a grand jesting tournament that would bring the realm together in a celebration of wit and mirth.

Excited by the prospect of a peaceful resolution, Tyrione penned letters to the great families of Jesteroos, inviting them to participate in the tournament. He hoped that by fostering camaraderie and laughter among them, they could forge alliances and friendships that would ultimately lead to the Irony Throne's rightful ruler.

In the cave of the Punder Master, Danyslack mustered all of her strength and wit, delivering a pun so powerful and clever that it brought the Punder Master to his knees. As he conceded defeat, the Punder Master relinquished control of the legendary rubber chickens to Danyslack, acknowledging her as their rightful wielder.

With the rubber chickens in her possession, Danyslack knew that the Irony Throne was within her grasp. She and Sir Jorah Memeont set off for Jesteroos, their hearts filled with hope and determination.

Word of the jesting tournament spread throughout Jesteroos, and excitement filled the air as families prepared their most hilarious jests, puns, and jokes. In Winterjests, Arya Snark redoubled her efforts in her training with Syri-Haha Forel, eager to represent her family in the tournament and prove her worth as a warrior of laughter.

As the day of the tournament drew near, the families of Jesteroos made their way to Pun's Landing, unaware of the challenges and surprises that awaited them. In the Game of Groans, laughter could unite or divide, and the future of the realm hung in the balance.

As the competitors took to the stage, the air was thick with anticipation. Tyrione Lannist-haha looked out at the gathered crowd, hoping that his gamble would pay off and that laughter would prove to be the key to uniting the realm.

One by one, the jesters and pun-masters took to the stage, delivering their most hilarious material. The audience roared with laughter, tears streaming down their faces as they reveled in the merriment.

As the tournament continued, it became clear that the true battle for the Irony Throne was not one of swords and blood, but of wit and laughter. And as the families of Jesteroos united in the spirit of humor, the realm began to heal, laughter ringing out like a beacon of hope in the darkness.

For in the Game of Groans, laughter was the key to victory, and those who mastered its power would rule the Irony Throne.

Chapter 4: The Battle of Wits

As the Punder Walkers drew closer, the people of Jesteroos looked to their leaders for guidance and protection. United by the spirit of laughter and the legacy of Neddard Snark, the great houses of the realm came together to form a coalition, pledging their loyalty to the cause of humor and unity.

Led by Neddard Snark, the forces of Jesteroos prepared for battle, honing their skills in wit and wordplay. Training camps were set up across the realm, where jesters and pun-masters shared their knowledge and expertise with the soldiers, transforming them into an army of laughter and mirth.

The battle against the Punder Walkers would not be won with steel and fire, but with wit and humor. In preparation for the inevitable clash, Neddard Snark devised a daring plan – a grand tournament of jest, where the champions of laughter from each house would face off against the Punder Walkers in a battle of wits and wordplay.

As the day of the tournament drew near, the people of Jesteroos gathered in Pun's Landing, the site of the upcoming battle. In the shadow of the Irony Throne, a grand amphitheater was constructed, a stage upon which the fate of the realm would be decided.

The tournament began with a series of duels, as the jesters and pun-masters of Jesteroos faced off against the Punder Walkers, their words and wit serving as their weapons. The air was filled with laughter and tension, as the champions of the realm fought valiantly to defend their home.

It was during the final round of the tournament that Neddard Snark took the stage, facing off against the leader of the Punder Walkers – the Night Punder. As the two opponents traded quips and puns, the fate of the realm hung in the balance, the outcome of the battle hinging on the strength of their wit and humor.

In the end, it was Neddard Snark who emerged victorious, his unbeatable combination of wit, timing, and charm winning over the judges and the hearts of the people. As the crowd erupted in laughter and applause, the Punder Walkers retreated, their power diminished by the indomitable spirit of humor that coursed through the realm.

With the threat of the Punder Walkers vanquished, the people of Jesteroos rejoiced, celebrating their victory with laughter and mirth. The great houses of the realm stood united, their bonds of friendship and loyalty forged in the fires of battle and the spirit of laughter.

The legacy of Neddard Snark lived on, his name becoming synonymous with the triumph of humor and the power of laughter to heal and unite. As the realm of Jesteroos continued to grow and prosper, the people looked to the example set by Neddard Snark, embracing the spirit of humor and unity that had brought them together and saved their world from darkness and despair.

In the years that followed, the story of Neddard Snark and the Battle of Wits was passed down through the generations, a timeless tale of courage, friendship, and the indomitable power of laughter. And as long as the people of Jesteroos continued to laugh and share their stories, the legacy of Neddard Snark would live on, a testament to the enduring spirit of the Game of Groans.

Chapter 5: A Feast for Laughs

As the jesting tournament in Pun's Landing continued, the spirit of laughter and camaraderie began to take hold of the families of Jesteroos. Bitter rivalries and long-standing feuds seemed to melt away in the face of the realm's most hilarious jokes and puns, replaced by a sense of unity and shared mirth.

Tyrione Lannist-haha watched the transformation with a mixture of relief and pride, hopeful that the power of laughter could truly bring peace to Jesteroos. But even as the spirit of unity grew stronger, Tyrione knew that the true test still lay ahead – the ultimate battle of wits to determine who would sit upon the Irony Throne.

Meanwhile, in Winterjests, Arya Snark had completed her training with Syri-Haha Forel and set off for Pun's Landing to represent her family in the jesting tournament. As she made her way south, her heart swelled with excitement and anticipation, eager to prove herself as a master of the Comedic Dance.

In the deserts of Es-Slack, Danyslack Targroan and Sir Jorah Memeont crossed the Giggling Wastes, their hearts set on claiming the Irony Throne with the power of the legendary rubber chickens. As they approached the shores of Jesteroos, they could feel the laughter that echoed across the realm, and they knew that their destiny was drawing near.

Back in Pun's Landing, the jesting tournament reached its climactic final round, with jesters and pun-masters from every corner of Jesteroos battling for the title of Champion of Laughter. The air was thick with the energy of competition, and the laughter that filled the streets was a testament to the power of humor.

As the final competitors took to the stage, the gathered crowd held their breath, waiting to see who would emerge victorious. The laughter that followed was like a tidal wave, washing over the audience and leaving them breathless with mirth.

In the end, it was Arya Snark, with her expertly honed skills in the Comedic Dance, who was crowned the Champion of Laughter. As she took her place on the stage, her family beaming with pride, it seemed as though the realm of Jesteroos had found its rightful ruler.

But as the celebrations continued, Danyslack Targroan arrived in Pun's Landing, the legendary rubber chickens in her possession. She strode through the streets, her eyes filled with determination, and challenged Arya Snark to a final, decisive battle of wits and wordplay.

The people of Pun's Landing gathered to witness the historic showdown, their hearts torn between the two formidable contenders. As Danyslack and Arya exchanged puns, jests, and jokes, it became clear that the fate of the Irony Throne would be decided by the slimmest of margins.

As the sun began to set, Arya and Danyslack stood facing each other, their voices hoarse from hours of laughter and wordplay. The gathered crowd watched in awe, their hearts pounding with anticipation.

In that final moment, as the laughter of the realm hung in the balance, it was Arya Snark who delivered the decisive blow – a pun so powerful and hilarious that even Danyslack could not help but laugh. And with that, the battle for the Irony Throne was won, and the people of Jesteroos knew that they had found their true queen.

GAME OF GROANS: THE IRONY THRONE

As Arya took her rightful place upon the Irony Throne, the realm of Jesteroos erupted in celebration. The power of laughter had united them, and for the first time in many years, the people of the realm knew peace and unity. Tyrione Lannist-haha looked on with pride, his dream of a realm brought together through laughter finally realized.

Danyslack Targroan, having been bested in the battle of wits, bowed before Arya Snark, pledging her loyalty and her legendary rubber chickens to the new ruler of Jesteroos. The two formidable women, once rivals, now stood united, their shared love of laughter and wit forging an unbreakable bond between them.

Under Arya's rule, the Irony Throne became a symbol of laughter and unity, and the people of Jesteroos thrived in a realm filled with mirth and joy. Jesters and pun-masters from all corners of the land were welcomed at court, their hilarious jokes and witty wordplay celebrated and cherished.

Jon Snowman, having successfully defended the realm from the Punder Walkers, returned to Winterjests to join his family in their newfound happiness. Reunited with Arya, he marveled at her growth and the mastery of the Comedic Dance she had achieved.

As the years passed, the realm of Jesteroos continued to flourish under Arya's rule. The power of laughter had triumphed over the darkness and bitterness that had once plagued the land, and the Irony Throne stood as a testament to the unifying force of humor.

And so, in a land where laughter had once been a weapon, it became a force for good, healing old wounds and forging new friendships. The Game of Groans had been won, and the people of Jesteroos knew that their future was brighter and more hilarious than they could have ever imagined.

For in the Game of Groans, laughter was the key to victory, and those who embraced its power would always find a reason to smile.

Chapter 6: The Laughter That Never Ends

The years that followed the crowning of Arya Snark as the ruler of Jesteroos were filled with laughter and joy. Under her wise and witty leadership, the realm flourished, and the Irony Throne became a beacon of unity and happiness.

In the great hall of Pun's Landing, Queen Arya held regular jesting tournaments, encouraging friendly competition between the families of Jesteroos. These events served to strengthen the bonds between the families and foster an atmosphere of camaraderie, where laughter reigned supreme.

Danyslack Targroan, now Arya's most trusted advisor and friend, continued her own journey of learning and growth. She traveled the realm, seeking out the greatest pun-masters and jesters, gathering their knowledge and honing her own skills in the art of humor. Through her travels, she became a legend in her own right, spreading laughter and joy wherever she went.

Jon Snowman, proud of his sister's accomplishments and the peace she had brought to Jesteroos, devoted himself to the Night's Chuckle, ensuring that the threat of the Punder Walkers remained a distant memory. Under his guidance, the Night's Chuckle transformed into an organization that not only guarded the realm against supernatural threats but also promoted laughter and happiness across Jesteroos.

Tyrione Lannist-haha, the man whose dream of laughter and unity had set the events of the Game of Groans in motion, served as Queen Arya's Hand. His quick wit and keen intellect proved invaluable in guiding the realm through times of both laughter and hardship.

As the realm of Jesteroos basked in the golden age of laughter, the people came to understand the true power of humor. No longer a weapon to be wielded in bitter conflict, laughter became a force that brought them together, uniting them in a shared appreciation for the joy and happiness that humor could bring.

And while the Irony Throne remained a symbol of power and authority, it also stood as a testament to the incredible journey that had brought the realm of Jesteroos to this new era of peace and laughter. From the icy reaches of the north to the sun-kissed shores of the south, the laughter that echoed across the land was a constant reminder of the unbreakable bonds that had been forged in the fires of the Game of Groans.

As the years turned to decades and the decades to centuries, the laughter that had once seemed so fragile and fleeting grew stronger and more enduring. The people of Jesteroos carried the legacy of Queen Arya Snark and her fellow champions of laughter in their hearts, ensuring that the laughter that had brought them together would never fade.

And so, in the realm of Jesteroos, the laughter that had begun with a dream and a hope for unity continued to ring out, a constant reminder of the power of humor to heal, to unite, and to bring happiness to all who embraced it.

Generations came and went, and the tales of Queen Arya Snark, Danyslack Targroan, Jon Snowman, and Tyrione Lannist-haha grew into legends that were shared across the realm of Jesteroos. Their stories of laughter, unity, and triumph inspired countless others to pursue lives filled with humor and wit.

In the shadow of the Irony Throne, the jesting tournaments continued to be held, honoring the legacy of Queen Arya and her fellow champions of laughter. Competitors from all corners of the realm gathered to showcase their wit and skill, eager to prove themselves worthy of their ancestors' humor and wisdom.

As the centuries passed, the realm of Jesteroos remained a land filled with laughter, where humor was cherished and celebrated. The once-bitter rivalries between the great families of the realm were now the stuff of jest and mirth, their battles replaced by friendly competitions of wit and wordplay.

In the far reaches of the north, the Night's Chuckle continued to stand watch over the realm, their vigilance a testament to the strength and resilience of the people of Jesteroos. Led by a long line of Snowman descendants, the organization spread laughter and joy throughout the land, ensuring that the legacy of Jon Snowman and his fellow defenders of the realm would never be forgotten.

The teachings of Danyslack Targroan lived on through the centuries, as the art of wielding rubber chickens and mastering the power of humor was passed down from generation to generation. Aspiring jesters and pun-masters traveled to the farthest corners of the realm to learn from the descendants of the legendary Danyslack, their hearts filled with hope and determination.

In the bustling streets of Pun's Landing, the spirit of Tyrione Lannist-haha endured, his name synonymous with wisdom, laughter, and unity. As the Hand of the Irony Throne, he had guided Jesteroos through countless challenges, always believing in the power of laughter to heal and unite the realm.

And as the laughter echoed across the realm, the people of Jesteroos knew that they were part of a great legacy – a legacy of laughter, unity, and triumph. They carried the stories of their ancestors in their hearts, sharing them with each new generation, ensuring that the spirit of the Game of Groans would live on.

For in the realm of Jesteroos, laughter was the greatest treasure, a gift that could be shared and enjoyed by all who embraced it. And as the laughter rang out across the land, it carried with it a promise – a promise that the lessons of the past would continue to guide the people of Jesteroos, uniting them in laughter, love, and hope.

And so, in the Game of Groans, laughter remained the ultimate victory, a testament to the power of humor and the indomitable spirit of the people of Jesteroos. And as long as laughter echoed through the realm, the legacy of Queen Arya Snark, Danyslack Targroan, Jon Snowman, and Tyrione Lannist-haha would live on – a reminder of the laughter, unity, and triumph that had once seemed like a distant dream, now etched forever in the heart of Jesteroos.

For in the Game of Groans, laughter was the ultimate victory, and those who held it close would always find a reason to smile.

As the centuries turned into millennia, the realm of Jesteroos continued to evolve, embracing new ideas and innovations that enriched the lives of its people. The spirit of laughter and unity that had been forged in the fires of the Game of Groans remained strong, guiding the people through times of change and uncertainty.

A new era dawned in Jesteroos, a renaissance of jest and mirth, as the art of humor expanded and flourished in ways that would have astounded the legendary Queen Arya Snark, Danyslack Targroan, Jon Snowman, and Tyrione Lannist-haha. From the bustling streets of Pun's Landing to the windswept shores of the Iron Islands, laughter and wit reigned supreme, uniting the people in a celebration of life and joy.

Throughout the realm, schools of humor were established, dedicated to teaching the ancient arts of wit and wordplay to new generations of aspiring jesters and pun-masters. These institutions became centers of learning and laughter, where the spirit of Queen Arya and her fellow champions of laughter lived on in the hearts and minds of those who walked their halls.

In the far north, the Night's Chuckle continued their eternal vigil, guarding the realm from the threat of the Punder Walkers and other dangers that lurked in the shadows. Under the leadership of the Snowman family, the organization embraced the renaissance of jest, incorporating the latest innovations and ideas into their training and tactics.

The descendants of Danyslack Targroan traveled the world, spreading the art of wielding rubber chickens and mastering the power of humor to new lands and cultures. Their journey was a testament to the enduring legacy of their ancestor, who had once crossed the Giggling Wastes in search of the legendary rubber chickens that would change the course of history.

As the renaissance of jest continued to shape the realm, the Irony Throne remained a symbol of unity and laughter, a testament to the power of humor to heal and unite the people of Jesteroos. The rulers who sat upon the throne were guided by the wisdom and wit of their ancestors, ensuring that the spirit of the Game of Groans would never fade from the hearts and minds of the people.

In the streets and markets of Pun's Landing, laughter echoed through the air, as jesters and pun-masters plied their trade, bringing smiles to the faces of all who passed by. The spirit of Tyrione Lannist-haha lived on in the city he had once called home, a constant reminder of the power of laughter to bridge the divide between even the bitterest of enemies.

And as the laughter rang out across the realm, the people of Jesteroos knew that they were part of a great legacy – a legacy of laughter, unity, and triumph that had begun with a dream and a hope for a better world. They carried the stories of their ancestors in their hearts, sharing them with each new generation, ensuring that the spirit of the Game of Groans would live on.

For in the realm of Jesteroos, laughter was the ultimate victory, a testament to the power of humor and the indomitable spirit of the people. And as long as laughter echoed through the realm, the legacy of Queen Arya Snark, Danyslack Targroan, Jon Snowman, and Tyrione Lannist-haha would live on – a reminder of the laughter, unity, and triumph that had once seemed like a distant dream, now etched forever in the heart of Jesteroos.

Chapter 7: The Festival of Folly

The Festival of Folly was a carefully orchestrated affair, with events and attractions spread throughout Pun's Landing. The streets were adorned with colorful banners and streamers, and the air was filled with the sweet scent of roasted almonds and honeycakes, as merchants and food vendors set up stalls to cater to the bustling crowds.

Among the memorable characters who gathered for the Festival of Folly, there was Ser Gigglesworth, the jousting jester, known for his uncanny ability to unseat his opponents with his razor-sharp wit and impeccably timed jokes. There was also Lady Bellylaugh, a renowned pun-mistress, who could weave intricate tapestries of wordplay that left her audience in stitches.

Another notable character was the enigmatic Whistling Wizard, a traveling magician whose dazzling displays of illusion were accompanied by a repertoire of side-splitting anecdotes that never failed to amaze and amuse. The mysterious performer was said to be a distant descendant of Danyslack Targroan, and many believed he had inherited her legendary talent for humor and spectacle.

Throughout the week-long celebration, a series of events took place, each showcasing a different aspect of humor and wit. There were jesting duels, where opponents faced off in battles of wits, trading jokes and quips in an effort to make each other laugh. The first one to laugh lost the duel, while the winner advanced to the next round.

One of the most anticipated events was the Punderdome, a grand arena where pun-masters from across the realm gathered to test their skills against one another. Contestants were given a topic, and they had to come up with as many puns as possible within a set time limit. The puns were then judged based on their cleverness and originality, with the winners advancing to the next round until a Punderdome Champion was crowned.

The Festival of Folly also featured a Giggling Gala, a glamorous ball where jesters, pun-masters, and the highborn elite of Jesteroos gathered for a night of laughter and dancing. The attendees were encouraged to wear their most amusing attire, and the evening was filled with games, riddles, and performances by some of the realm's most talented jesters.

One of the highlights of the festival was the Prankster's Parade, a procession through the streets of Pun's Landing, where performers showed off their skills in slapstick comedy, acrobatics, and physical humor. The parade was led by none other than Ser Gigglesworth, who rode atop his trusty steed, Bananapeel, delighting the crowds with his antics and leaving a trail of laughter in his wake.

The culmination of the Festival of Folly was the Grand Tournament of Jest. The competition took place in a grand amphitheater, where contestants faced off in a series of challenges that tested their wit, humor, and creativity. The tournament was a grueling test of skill and endurance, with only the most tenacious and talented jesters making it through to the final round.

In the end, it was Ser Gigglesworth who emerged victorious, his unbeatable combination of wit, timing, and charm winning over the judges and earning him the title of Champion of Folly. As the newly crowned champion, Ser Gigglesworth was granted the honor of performing for the ruler of Jesteroos, a moment that would forever be etched in the annals of history as a testament to the power of laughter and the indomitable spirit of the people of Jesteroos.

With the Festival of Folly, the realm celebrated its unique heritage, honoring the legacy of Queen Arya Snark, Danyslack Targroan, Jon Snowman, and Tyrione Lannisthaha. The laughter and unity that echoed throughout the streets of Pun's Landing during the festival were a testament to the power of humor to heal and unite the people of Jesteroos.

As the Festival of Folly drew to a close, the people of the realm returned to their homes, their hearts filled with laughter and fond memories of the week-long celebration. The spirit of the festival lived on, inspiring countless tales and songs that were shared around hearths and firesides, ensuring that the legacy of the Game of Groans would never fade from the hearts and minds of the people.

In the years that followed, the Festival of Folly became an annual event, a cherished tradition that brought people from all walks of life together to celebrate the unique heritage of Jesteroos and the power of laughter to heal and unite. Each year, the festival grew in size and scope, drawing people from far and wide to partake in the joyous celebrations and honor the legacy of the Game of Groans.

And as laughter continued to echo throughout the realm, the people of Jesteroos knew that they were part of a great legacy – a legacy of laughter, unity, and triumph that had begun with a dream and a hope for a better world. They carried the stories of their ancestors in their hearts, sharing them with each new generation, ensuring that the spirit of the Game of Groans would live on.

For in the realm of Jesteroos, laughter was the ultimate victory, a testament to the power of humor and the indomitable spirit of the people. And as long as laughter echoed through the realm, the legacy of Queen Arya Snark, Danyslack Targroan, Jon Snowman, and Tyrione Lannist-haha would live on – a reminder of the laughter, unity, and triumph that had once seemed like a distant dream, now etched forever in the heart of Jesteroos.

Chapter 8: Sersilly Lannist-hair

In the golden lands of Casterly Chuckle, the Lannist-hair family was known for their wealth, cunning, and, most of all, their luxurious locks of hair. Among the many members of this powerful house, Sersilly Lannist-hair stood out as a figure of both admiration and ridicule.

Born to Lord Tywin Lannist-hair and Lady Joanna, Sersilly was the eldest of the Lannist-hair siblings, and from a young age, she was groomed to be the embodiment of her family's power and prestige. As a child, Sersilly was trained in the arts of politics and courtly manners, learning the importance of wit and cunning from her father and the art of charm and persuasion from her mother.

However, it was her hair that truly set Sersilly apart. Blessed with a mane of lustrous golden curls, Sersilly was the envy of every noblewoman in the realm. She took great pride in her hair, spending countless hours grooming and styling it, often to the point of obsession.

Despite her beauty and grace, Sersilly's pride in her hair and her haughty demeanor earned her the ridicule of her peers. Unbeknownst to her, whispers of her vanity and frivolousness spread throughout Casterly Chuckle, and the once-admired Sersilly soon found herself the target of cruel jokes and nicknames.

Determined to prove herself as more than just her hair, Sersilly sought the counsel of her younger brother, Jamie Lannom-ster. A renowned chef and master of cooking puns, Jamie taught Sersilly the power of humor and wordplay, showing her how laughter could be used as both a weapon and a shield.

Armed with her newfound skills, Sersilly began to embrace her role as the butt of the joke, using her wit and cunning to turn the tables on her detractors. As her reputation for humor and wordplay grew, so too did her influence within the Lannist-hair family, as she proved herself to be a force to be reckoned with both in and out of the jesting arena.

It was during this time that Sersilly met King Baratheomnomnom, the gluttonous ruler of the neighboring lands. Intrigued by his love of feasting and humor, Sersilly forged a powerful alliance with the king, using her charm and wit to win him over. As their friendship blossomed, so too did the ties between their families, solidifying a partnership that would prove instrumental in the fight against the Punder Walkers.

When news of the impending threat reached Casterly Chuckle, Sersilly Lannist-hair was among the first to pledge her support to the cause. Alongside her family and her newfound allies, Sersilly stood ready to face the darkness that threatened the realm of Jesteroos, armed with the power of laughter and the indomitable spirit of the Lannist-hair family.

As the people of Jesteroos banded together to defeat the Punder Walkers, the story of Sersilly Lannist-hair served as a reminder of the power of humor to transform and empower. Her journey from vanity and ridicule to wit and cunning became a symbol of resilience and adaptability, ensuring that the legacy of Sersilly Lannist-hair would live on as an integral part of the Game of Groans.

Chapter 9: Squire Pycelle

In the bustling city of Pun's Landing, there lived a young man named Pycelle, whose life was destined to be intertwined with the fates of the great houses of Jesteroos. Born to a family of modest means, Pycelle showed an early aptitude for wordplay and humor, often entertaining his friends and family with his clever quips and jests.

Pycelle's talents did not go unnoticed, and at the age of sixteen, he was offered an apprenticeship under the renowned Jester of Pun's Landing, who served as the official entertainer for the Irony Throne. Under the Jester's tutelage, Pycelle honed his skills in humor and wit, learning the art of subtle wordplay and the power of laughter to charm and disarm.

As Pycelle's skills grew, so too did his reputation, and it was not long before he caught the eye of the Lannist-hair family, who saw in the young man a valuable ally and a potential pawn in their political games. Eager to rise through the ranks and prove his worth, Pycelle accepted the Lannist-hairs' offer to serve as their personal squire, a position that would bring him closer to the heart of power in Pun's Landing.

Though his days were filled with menial tasks and errands, Pycelle's evenings were spent in the company of the Lannist-hair siblings, where he entertained them with his humor and wit. As his connection with the family deepened, Pycelle found himself privy to the inner workings of the Lannist-hair's political machinations, witnessing firsthand the cunning and ruthlessness that defined their rise to power.

As the years went by, Pycelle became an indispensable member of the Lannist-hair household, his loyalty and discretion earning him the trust and respect of his patrons. Yet, as he grew closer to the heart of power, Pycelle also found himself ensnared in a web of intrigue and deception, his own ambition and loyalty tested by the shifting sands of the Game of Groans.

When the threat of the Punder Walkers began to loom over Jesteroos, Pycelle found himself faced with a difficult choice. As the Lannist-hairs pledged their support to the cause, Pycelle was torn between his loyalty to the family that had raised him from obscurity and his own growing sense of unease at their ruthless pursuit of power.

In the end, it was the memory of his humble beginnings and the lessons he had learned as a squire that guided Pycelle's decision. As the forces of Jesteroos united against the Punder Walkers, Pycelle chose to stand with his fellow jesters and pun-masters, using his skills in humor and wordplay to defend the realm and bring laughter to the people of Jesteroos.

The story of Squire Pycelle serves as a reminder that even the humblest among us can make a difference in the great game of life. His journey from apprentice jester to the squire of a powerful house illustrates the power of laughter and wit to bridge the gap between social classes and unite the people of Jesteroos in the face of darkness and despair.

Chapter 10: Sir Jorah Memeont

In the rolling hills of Bear-sland, the Memeont family was known for their fierce loyalty, steadfast honor, and, most notably, their penchant for creating the most uproarious memes in all of Jesteroos. From their ancestral seat of Memehall, the Memeonts used humor and satire to unite their people, forging a strong bond that had endured for generations.

Among the members of this noble house, Sir Jorah Memeont was a man of great respect and a peculiar destiny. Born to Lord Jeor Memeont and Lady Alys, Jorah was raised with a strong sense of duty and honor, instilled in him by his father, the Warden of the Memes. Yet, it was his mother who first introduced him to the power of laughter, regaling him with stories of Jesteroos and the countless memes that had brought joy to the realm.

As Jorah grew into a young man, he began to explore the world of humor and satire, his curiosity driving him to seek out the most skilled meme-makers and pun-masters across the realm. It was during his travels that Jorah first encountered the art of meme-making, a practice that combined his love of humor with his passion for honor and duty.

Embracing this newfound skill, Jorah returned to Bear-sland and began crafting memes that celebrated the virtues of loyalty, courage, and wit. His creations quickly gained popularity, spreading throughout the realm and earning him the title of Sir Jorah Memeont, the Knight of the Meme.

However, Jorah's rising fame came at a cost. As his memes began to attract the attention of rival houses, he found himself embroiled in a web of intrigue and deception, his honor and loyalty tested by the ever-shifting alliances and betrayals of the Game of Groans.

It was during this tumultuous time that Jorah met Danyslack Targroan, the exiled princess of the fallen House Targroan. Intrigued by her vision of a united Jesteroos, where laughter and joy could heal the wounds of the past, Jorah pledged his service to Danyslack, vowing to help her reclaim her family's lost legacy and restore peace to the realm.

As Danyslack's most trusted advisor, Jorah stood by her side through thick and thin, using his skills in humor and meme-making to rally the people of Jesteroos to her cause. Together, they embarked on a journey that would take them across the realm, forging alliances and confronting foes in their quest to bring laughter and unity to a fractured world.

The story of Sir Jorah Memeont serves as a testament to the power of humor and the resilience of the human spirit. In his journey from the Knight of the Meme to the trusted advisor of the Mother of Punder Dragons, Jorah proves that laughter can bridge the gap between honor and duty, forging bonds that transcend the rivalries and conflicts of the Game of Groans.

Chapter 11: Jon Snowman

In the cold and unforgiving lands of the Frost, the inhabitants had learned to find solace and warmth in laughter, their spirits sustained by the power of humor and the bonds of camaraderie. Among these hardy folk, a young man named Jon Snowman would rise to prominence, his wit and wordplay capturing the hearts of his people and shaping the destiny of Jesteroos.

Born under mysterious circumstances, Jon Snowman was taken in by Lord Eddark Snark of Winterjoke, a man renowned for his sense of humor and his unwavering loyalty to the Irony Throne. Raised alongside Lord Snark's trueborn children, Jon was treated as a member of the family, his natural talent for puns and jests nurtured and encouraged by his adoptive father.

As Jon grew older, he began to question his origins, the whispers and sideways glances of his fellow Frostfolk a constant reminder of the secret that lay hidden in his past. Driven by a desire to find his place in the world, Jon decided to join the Night's Jest, a legendary order of jesters and pun-masters dedicated to defending the realm from the threat of the Punder Walkers.

At the Wall of Wit, a colossal structure that stretched across the northern border of Jesteroos, Jon Snowman quickly earned the respect and admiration of his fellow jesters. His clever quips and unerring sense of humor made him a natural leader, and it wasn't long before he was elevated to the rank of Lord Commander of the Night's Jest.

As the shadow of the Punder Walkers loomed ever larger, Jon Snowman found himself at the forefront of the battle to save Jesteroos from the darkness that threatened to engulf it. United by their love of laughter and their shared sense of duty, the men and women of the Night's Jest stood together, determined to defend the realm with their wit and their words.

It was during this time that Jon Snowman discovered the truth of his parentage, a revelation that would change the course of his life and the fate of Jesteroos forever. As the long-lost son of Danyslack Targroan and Prince Rhae-Gar the Jester, Jon found himself torn between his duty to the Night's Jest and his newfound loyalty to the Mother of Punder Dragons.

Faced with an impossible choice, Jon Snowman chose to embrace both his heritage and his sense of duty, uniting the forces of Jesteroos in their battle against the Punder Walkers. As the armies of laughter and light clashed with the dark forces of pun and despair, Jon Snowman stood as a symbol of hope, his wit and humor a beacon in the darkness.

The story of Jon Snowman serves as a reminder that even in the face of overwhelming odds, laughter and camaraderie can triumph over adversity. His journey from the Frost to the heart of Jesteroos illustrates the power of humor and wit to unite the realm and bring light to the darkest corners of the world.

Epilogue: A Realm United in Laughter

In the aftermath of the great Punder Walker battle, the lands of Jesteroos found themselves united by the power of humor, wit, and the indomitable spirit of their heroes. The Irony Throne, once a symbol of strife and conflict, had been transformed into a seat of unity and mirth, the laughter of the realm echoing through its halls.

King Jon Snowman and Queen Danyslack Targroan, their love for laughter and each other proving stronger than any obstacle, ruled over Jesteroos with a kind and light-hearted hand. The once-frosty relationship between the Frost and the rest of the realm had thawed, thanks to Jon's warmth and wit.

At the Wall of Wit, the Night's Jest continued to hone their puns and jokes, ensuring that the people of Jesteroos would always have a reason to chuckle in the face of adversity. The Punder Dragons soared through the skies, their laughter-inducing breath a constant reminder of the power of humor to overcome even the darkest of foes.

The bards and jesters of Jesteroos regaled the people with tales of their heroes' adventures, the stories of Jon Snowman, Danyslack Targroan, Sersilly Lannist-hair, and the others bringing laughter and inspiration to all who heard them. Among these legendary figures, the story of the Night's Jest and the Punder Walkers held a special place, the epic wordplay and pun-filled battles a testament to the power of laughter in the face of darkness.

And so, the realm of Jesteroos entered a new era of unity and mirth, the once-bitter rivalries and conflicts of the Game of Groans giving way to laughter and camaraderie. From the icy reaches of the Frost to the sun-kissed shores of Dorne, the people of Jesteroos stood together, their hearts filled with joy and their voices raised in laughter.

As the sun set on the Irony Throne, a new dawn began for the people of Jesteroos, their future filled with puns, jokes, and the promise of a brighter, more laughter-filled world. For in the end, it was not the clash of swords or the roar of dragons that had saved the realm, but the power of laughter and the indomitable spirit of those who dared to believe in the magic of humor.

In Jesteroos, laughter truly was king. And as the people of the realm looked to the future, they knew that their united voices, filled with mirth and joy, would forever echo through the annals of history, a testament to the power of laughter to unite a realm and heal the wounds of the past.

Bonus Content

Prequel: The Jest That Brought the Realm Together

Once upon a time in the realm of Jesteroos, laughter and merriment filled the air, as the people of the land found unity in the warmth of shared jokes and the joy of humor. It was an era when the great houses stood side by side, bound together by the spirit of jest and the bonds of camaraderie.

In this time of unity, a great festival was held in the capital city of King's Landing, a celebration of laughter and wit that drew jesters and pun-masters from all corners of the realm. From the icy reaches of the Frost to the sun-kissed shores of Dorne, the people of Jesteroos gathered to share in the mirth and joy of the occasion, their differences forgotten in the face of their shared love of laughter.

The highlight of the festival was to be a grand competition, a contest of wit and humor that would see the finest jesters and pun-masters of the realm pitted against one another in a battle of words and laughter. The winner of the contest would be awarded the title of Grand Jester, a position of great honor and prestige that would secure their place in the annals of Jesteroos history.

As the day of the contest approached, the excitement in King's Landing reached a fever pitch, the people of the realm eagerly anticipating the spectacle that was to come. The great houses, eager to demonstrate their prowess in the art of jest, each selected a champion to represent them in the competition, their hopes and dreams riding on the shoulders of these skilled wordsmiths.

Among the champions was a young jester named Rolly Gigglewaters, a man of humble origins who had risen to prominence thanks to his quick wit and his uncanny ability to craft puns that left his audience in fits of laughter. Representing House Snark, Rolly was determined to win the title of Grand Jester, not only for the glory of his house but for the unity of the realm itself.

As the contest began, the champions of Jesteroos took turns displaying their skill and humor, their jests and jibes filling the air with laughter and delight. Yet, as the competition wore on, it became clear that Rolly Gigglewaters was a cut above the rest, his puns and wordplay weaving a tapestry of humor that left the audience breathless with laughter.

In the final round of the competition, Rolly stood before the gathered crowd, his eyes filled with determination and his heart buoyed by the laughter that surrounded him. With a deep breath, he delivered his final jest, a pun so masterful and unexpected that it brought the entire realm together in a moment of shared mirth and joy.

"Why did the dragon refuse to eat jesters?" Rolly asked, a twinkle in his eye as the crowd leaned forward in anticipation. "Because they tasted too punny!"

As the laughter rippled through the audience, Rolly Gigglewaters knew that he had achieved something truly special, his jest a testament to the power of humor to unite a realm and heal the wounds of the past. Crowned as the Grand Jester, Rolly pledged to use his newfound title to promote laughter and unity throughout Jesteroos, his heart filled with hope for the future.

And so, in the golden age of laughter, a humble jester named Rolly Gigglewaters showed the people of Jesteroos the true power of humor and the indomitable spirit of those who dared to believe in the magic of laughter. As the shadows of the Game of Groans began to gather on the horizon, Rolly's jest served as a reminder that laughter, in all its forms, had the power to change the world and bring people together, no matter the challenges they faced.

Rolly Gigglewaters' legacy lived on in the hearts and minds of the people of Jesteroos, his name forever synonymous with the unity and laughter that once defined the realm. As the winds of change blew across the land and the once-united people of Jesteroos found themselves caught in the bitter struggle of the Game of Groans, the memory of Rolly's jest served as a beacon of hope, a reminder of the power of laughter to overcome even the darkest of times.

And though the Age of Laughter would eventually give way to the trials and tribulations of the Irony Throne, the story of Rolly Gigglewaters and his jest would never be forgotten, a shining example of the resilience and spirit that had once brought the realm together and could do so again.

For in the realm of Jesteroos, laughter was a force to be reckoned with, a weapon capable of piercing even the thickest of armors and the most hardened of hearts. And as the people of the land looked to the future, their hearts filled with hope and their voices raised in laughter, they knew that the spirit of Rolly Gigglewaters and the Age of Laughter would forever be a part of their shared history, a testament to the power of humor to unite a realm and bring light to the darkest corners of the world.

Sequel: The Return of the Grand Jester

Years had passed since the great Punder Walker battle, and the realm of Jesteroos was now united by the power of humor, wit, and the indomitable spirit of their heroes. The Irony Throne, once a symbol of strife and conflict, had been transformed into a seat of unity and mirth. The laughter of the realm echoed through its halls, as the once-bitter rivalries and conflicts gave way to laughter and camaraderie.

In this time of peace and unity, it was decided that a grand celebration should be held in honor of the heroes who had fought so bravely to restore laughter to the realm. From every corner of Jesteroos, people gathered to share in the joy and laughter that now defined their world, the spirit of merriment a testament to the power of humor to heal the wounds of the past.

At the heart of the celebration was a contest of wit and humor, a competition that would see the finest jesters and pun-masters of the realm pitted against one another in a battle of words and laughter. The prize for the victor was the title of the new Grand Jester, a position of honor and prestige that had been vacant since the days of Rolly Gigglewaters, the legendary jester who had once united the realm with a single, masterful jest.

As the contest began, the champions of Jesteroos took turns displaying their skill and humor, their jests and jibes filling the air with laughter and delight. Among the competitors was a young jester named Witty Wobblequill, a descendant of the great Rolly Gigglewaters himself. Armed with a sharp wit and an unshakable belief in the power of laughter, Witty was determined to follow in the footsteps of his ancestor and claim the title of Grand Jester for himself.

The competition was fierce, as jesters from across the realm traded puns and jokes in a battle of wits that left the audience in stitches. As the final round approached, it was clear that Witty Wobblequill had emerged as the favorite, his natural talent for humor and his unwavering dedication to the spirit of laughter capturing the hearts and minds of the people of Jesteroos.

Standing before the gathered crowd, Witty knew that this was his moment, his chance to secure not only the title of Grand Jester but the unity and laughter of the realm itself. Drawing upon the wisdom and humor passed down through generations of his family, he delivered a jest so powerful and unexpected that it brought the entire realm together in a moment of shared mirth and joy.

"What do you call a knight who always brings laughter to the realm?" Witty asked, his voice filled with the confidence and spirit of his ancestors. "A Sir-Prize!"

As the laughter rippled through the audience, Witty Wobblequill knew that he had achieved something truly special, his jest a testament to the power of humor to unite a realm and heal the wounds of the past. Crowned as the new Grand Jester, Witty pledged to use his newfound title to promote laughter and unity throughout Jesteroos, ensuring that the legacy of Rolly Gigglewaters and the Age of Laughter would live on for generations to come.

And so, in the realm of Jesteroos, the spirit of laughter and unity was reborn, a beacon of hope and joy that would forever light the way forward for the people of the land. For in the end, it was the laughter of their heroes and the unwavering belief in the power of humor that had saved the realm, a legacy that would endure for all time.

Made in the USA
Monee, IL
04 May 2025